This Walker book belongs to:

_____

_____

For Pat A.M.

For Jo and her family
and all the Jack Russells
they have loved S.R.

First published 2016
by Walker Books Ltd, 87 Vauxhall Walk,
London SE11 5HJ

This edition published 2017

2 4 6 8 10 9 7 5 3 1

Text © 2016 Amanda McCardie
Illustrations © 2016 Salvatore Rubbino

The right of Amanda McCardie and
Salvatore Rubbino to be identified as author and
illustrator respectively of this work has been asserted
by them in accordance with the Copyright,
Designs and Patents Act 1988

This book has been typeset in Clarendon T Light
and Keswick

Printed and bound in China

British Library Cataloguing in Publication Data:
a catalogue record for this book is available
from the British Library.

ISBN 978-1-4063-7347-9

www.walker.co.uk

Our Very Own
DOG

Amanda McCardie

illustrated by
Salvatore Rubbino

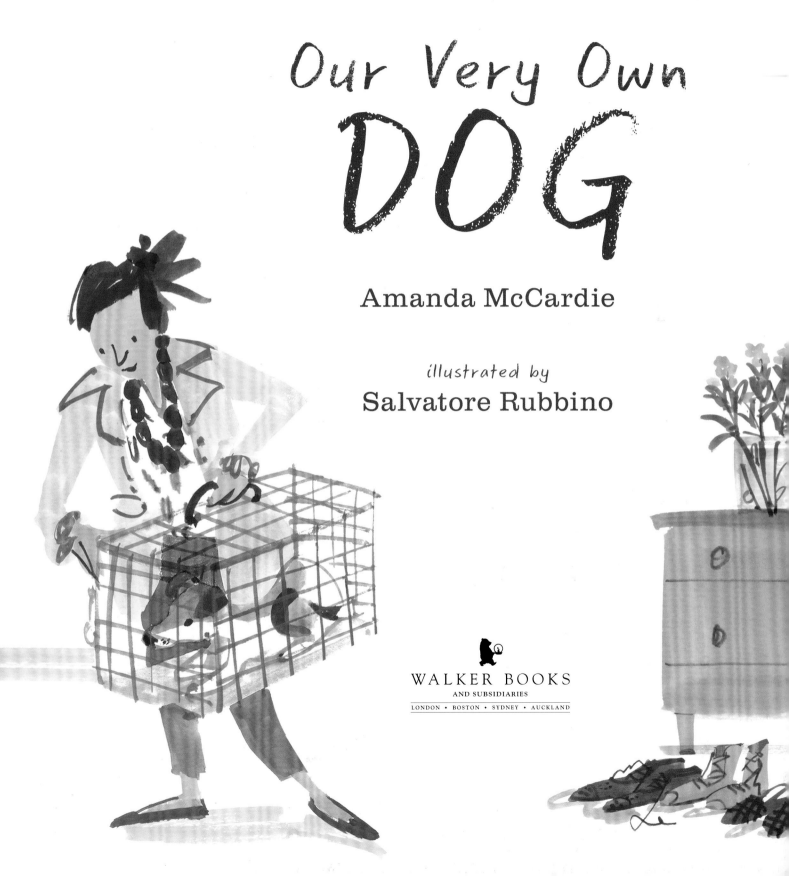

WALKER BOOKS
AND SUBSIDIARIES
LONDON • BOSTON • SYDNEY • AUCKLAND

A dog came to live with us
when I was four.

For a minute or two she sat by me.

Then she climbed right over my back and nuzzled

my hand with her cold wet nose.

Hello, Sophie!

Sophie had been living at a dogs' home.

Now she had her own home – with us.

We had things ready for our new dog:

a cosy bed and blankets,

bowls for food and water,

a toy to cuddle,

one to chew,

a ball, a lead

and a collar.

A chew toy is useful because dogs need to chew.
It's natural, calming and good for their teeth.

We fitted her collar and felt it with our fingers
to make sure it wasn't too tight.
It had a metal tag on it that
jingled as she walked.

There, Sophie!

A shy or nervous
dog may feel
threatened
if you look
too closely into
her face.

Sophie was shy of my father at first,
so he took care not to look in her eyes
or stroke her or get too close.

Instead, he spoke to her gently and made her the tastiest dinners.

Friendly voices relax dogs and help to build trust.

Soon she came to love him best of all.

Your vet can offer advice on how to provide your dog with a healthy diet. This may include dog treats for training - but not too many!

Being a dog, Sophie couldn't talk, but she learnt to understand

"Sit!"

"Stay!"

"Come!"

and "Heel!"

Training works best when it is kind, patient and the same every time.

A dog who walks "to heel" won't rush into a busy road.

She knew her own
name, Sophie ...

though she sometimes pretended not to.

A dog's whiskers
are useful "feelers".

And she always heard the word "*Walkies!*" even if you said it in a whisper.

Good dog-owners scoop poop!

Dogs should only be let off the lead if they can be trusted to come when they're called.

All dogs need regular exercise. Big dogs need the most.

14

We took Sophie walking every day so she could run and roll, sniff smells and meet other dogs.

There are more than 400 breeds of dog. Many dogs are a mixture of breeds.

Dogs are highly sociable animals who want lots of company.

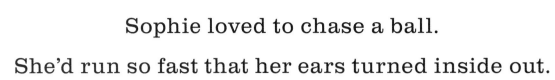

Sophie loved to chase a ball.

She'd run so fast that her ears turned inside out.

Go, Sophie!

She'd drop the ball
for you to throw –

then snatch it
up herself.

Dogs can't sweat to cool down the way we do (except on the pads of their paws).
Panting helps to cool them when they get hot.

Sophie could move quickly when she wanted to,
as we found out when she first
smelt sausages.

A dog's sense of smell is
one to ten thousand times
more sensitive than a person's.
Smells are important to dogs.

Hey, Sophie!

Those were for us!

Sophie enjoyed a tickle and a stroke, or a brush for those hard-to-reach itches.

A dog should have her own brush and comb for grooming.

Most dogs like to be stroked by their owners, but many don't want to be touched by strangers. Always ask the owner before you touch a dog.

But she wasn't keen on being washed.

She liked it better when we had baths.

Shoo, Sophie!

Sophie never minded getting dirty.
One day, she splashed through every puddle
in the park then shook out her fur to get dry.

Oh, Sophie!

Shaking is a highly efficient
way for a dog to get dry
– much quicker than a towel!

As we made our muddy way back home,

we passed a big sign that said DOG SHOW.

We only went to take a look.

We never meant to enter Sophie.

But Sophie wagged her tail
at the judge and gazed up
into his eyes.

Can you guess who
won the prize that day
for the friendliest dog?

25

It was Sophie!

27

Your Very Own Dog

If you ever think of getting a dog, you need to find out as much as you can about dogs and to work out which kind would best suit your family.

You can learn from books, dog owners, rescue centres, trainers and vets, and by watching and listening to the dogs you meet. Every bark, whine and whimper has a meaning. Dogs also "speak" with their bodies, eyes, ears and tails. A dog whose language you understand will be your friend for life.

friendly

happy

playful

How-ow-owl!

lonely

frightened

A Few Useful Books About Dogs

The Canine Commandments by Kendal Shepherd (Broadcast Books, 2007), *Complete Puppy and Dog Care* by Bruce Fogle with Patricia Holden White (Mitchell Beazley, 2014), *The Dog Expert* by Karen Bush with Dr D.G. Hessayon (Expert Books, 2010) and *Do Dogs Dream?* by Stanley Coren (W.W. Norton & Co, 2013).

Index

Look up the pages to find out about all these doggy things. Don't forget to look at both kinds of word - **this kind** and *this kind*.

Other books illustrated by Salvatore Rubbino:

A Walk in New York

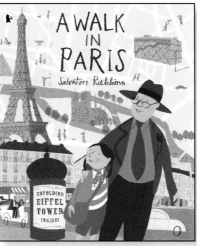

A Walk in Paris

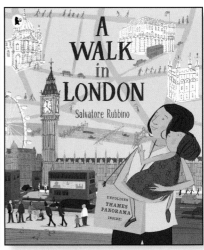

A Walk in London

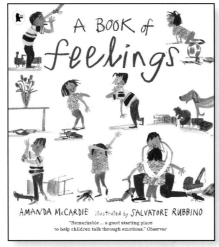

A Book of Feelings

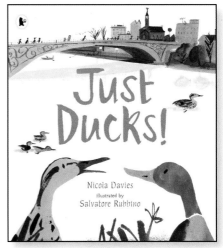

Just Ducks!

Available from all good booksellers

www.walker.co.uk